KU-430-643

ERIC MADDERN'S career as a singer/storyteller
of Aboriginal and Celtic myths and folk tales
has taken him touring all over Britain
with English Heritage. Born in South Australia
and educated in Britain, where he read psychology
and sociology at the University of Sheffield, he is now settled
in North Wales. His children's books include *Curious Clownfish*
and *Rainbow Bird*, both published by Frances Lincoln.

FRANÉ LESSAC is an internationally known
American artist who has exhibited her paintings
in London, Paris, New York and Los Angeles.
From film school in California she went on to study
Caribbean culture on the island of Montserrat.
Her first book for Frances Lincoln
was Barbara Ker Wilson's *The Turtle and the Island*.
She lives in West Australia with her husband
and two children.

Montem Primary School
Hornsey Road
London N7 7QT
Tel: 0171 272 6556
Fax: 0171 272 1838

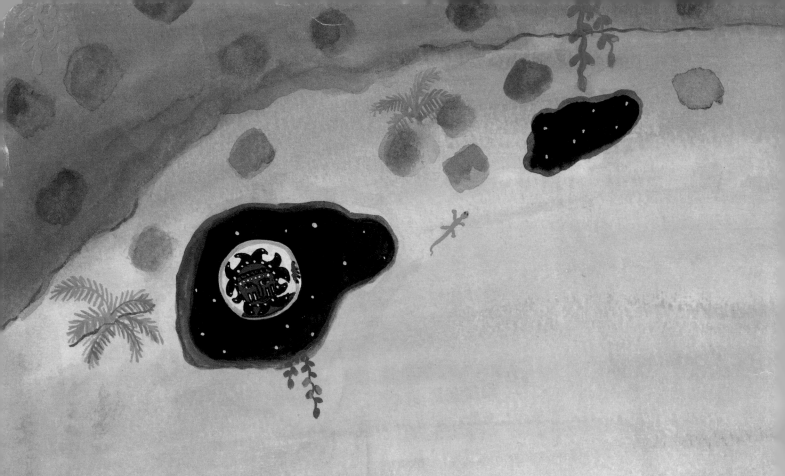

**For respect and goodwill
between the peoples of the Earth – E.M.
For Mark – F.L.**

The Fire Children copyright © Frances Lincoln Limited 1993
Text copyright © Eric Maddern 1993
This story is based on a West African creation myth
adapted from *Gods and Men: Myths and Legends from the World's Religions,*
retold by John R. Bailey, Kenneth McLeish and David Spearman
(Oxford University Press) 1981
Illustrations copyright © Frané Lessac 1993

First published in Great Britain in 1993 by
Frances Lincoln Limited, 4 Torriano Mews
Torriano Avenue, London NW5 2RZ

First paperback edition 1994

British Library Cataloguing in Publication Data
available on request

ISBN 0-7112-0783-6 hardback
ISBN 0-7112-0885-9 paperback

Set in Bembo Roman

Printed in Hong Kong

3 5 7 9 8 6 4

THE FIRE CHILDREN
A West African folk tale

Retold by Eric Maddern
Illustrated by Frané Lessac

FRANCES LINCOLN

Long ago Nyame, the great sky-god, lived alone in the wide blue sky. One day he took a basket and filled it with earth, trees, flowers, insects and birds, and he hung it in the sky. That basket was the Earth.

Then he made a round trapdoor in the sky so that he could climb down to visit the earth, with little holes so that the light could shine through when the trapdoor was shut. The trapdoor and holes were the moon and the stars.

One day Nyame was looking through his trapdoor moon admiring the Earth down below. But deep inside him two little spirit people were curious. They wanted to see what was going on.

So they climbed up Nyame's throat, into his mouth, over his tongue and were just looking through his teeth when he let out a tremendous sneeze.

The two spirit people, Kwaku Ananse and Aso Yaa,
went flying out through the trapdoor,
down,
down,
down,

and landed with a bump on the Earth.

They picked themselves up and looked around at the tall trees and hanging vines, the dark pools and splashing streams, the brilliant birds flashing through the leaves. Nearby they found a warm cave and decided to make it their home.

Each day they went outside to explore, to sing with the wind and dance with the falling leaves.

One day Aso Yaa was lonely, and she stayed at home in the cave. When Kwaku Ananse returned she had a big smile on her face.

"Oh Aso Yaa of many moods," he said, "when I left this morning you were sad. Now you are glowing like a hibiscus flower. What is it?"

"I have an idea," she said.

"Not another idea!" said Kwaku Ananse. "Last time you had an idea we were inside Nyame. Now look where we are!"

"Listen," said Aso Yaa. "It will not hurt you to listen."

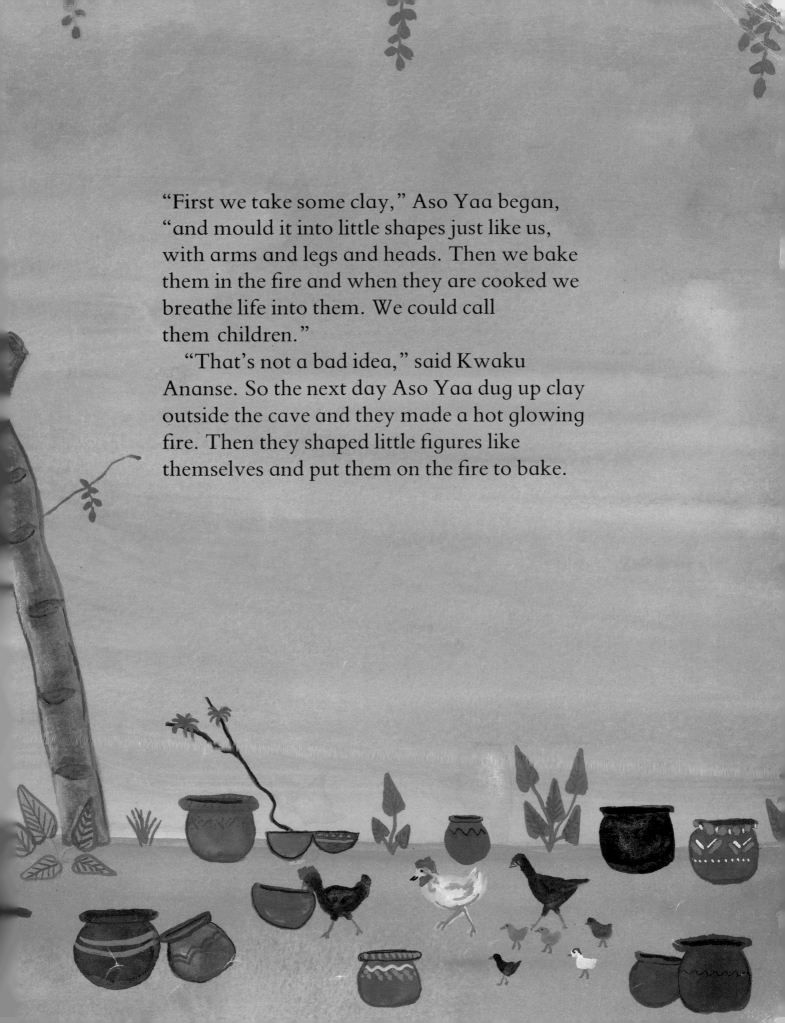

"First we take some clay," Aso Yaa began, "and mould it into little shapes just like us, with arms and legs and heads. Then we bake them in the fire and when they are cooked we breathe life into them. We could call them children."

"That's not a bad idea," said Kwaku Ananse. So the next day Aso Yaa dug up clay outside the cave and they made a hot glowing fire. Then they shaped little figures like themselves and put them on the fire to bake.

Suddenly, they heard crashing footsteps outside in the forest. Nyame had come to visit. Frightened that they were doing wrong, Kwaku Ananse and Aso Yaa snatched the little clay figures from the fire, wrapped them in leaves and hid them at the back of the cave.

Nyame's face appeared at the mouth of the cave.

"Well, my spirit people," he said, "are you enjoying my Earth?"

"Oh yes, Nyame," they replied.

"Are you being good?"

"Oh yes, Nyame," they answered, "we're being very good."

"Well, take good care of everything I have made," Nyame boomed, and then he disappeared.

Next day, Aso Yaa made a new batch of clay children, but no sooner had they begun to bake than Nyame was back again.

This time the spirit people had no time to take out the little figures. Instead, they stood in front of the fire hiding their work. And this time Nyame stayed talking for a long time. Maybe he suspected something. By the time he was gone, the clay children were baked quite black.

And so it went on. Every day they made more shapes and put them in the fire. And every day Nyame called to see them. Sometimes they heard him coming and were able to take the children out of the fire. Sometimes they had to leave them in the fire until he had gone.

But at last Nyame climbed back through the trapdoor moon and into the sky world above.

Then Kwaku Ananse and Aso Yaa spread out all the fire children. Some were hardly cooked at all and were white. Some were rosy pink, some honey yellow, some dusky red, some nut brown – and some midnight black. Kwaku Ananse and Aso Yaa loved them all, because they were their children.

Now the spirit people breathed life into the fire children. One by one they awoke, yawned, stretched and opened their eyes, just like children waking up in the morning. Then they stood up and went off to play.

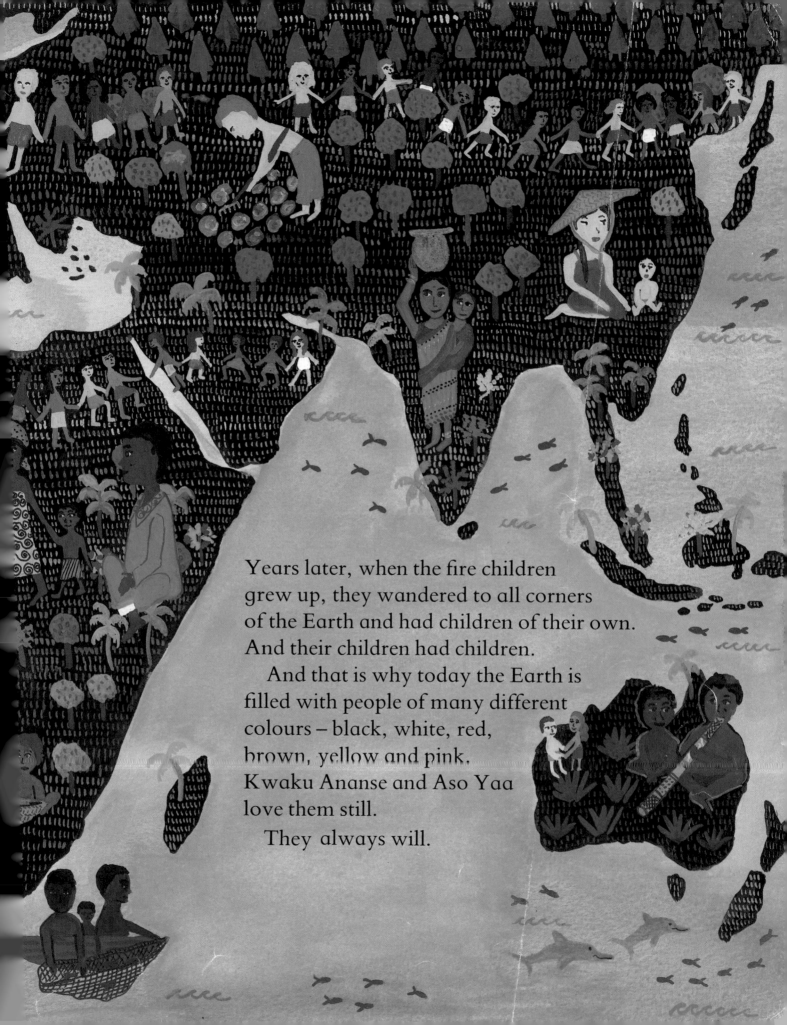

Years later, when the fire children grew up, they wandered to all corners of the Earth and had children of their own. And their children had children.

And that is why today the Earth is filled with people of many different colours – black, white, red, brown, yellow and pink. Kwaku Ananse and Aso Yaa love them still.

They always will.

MORE PICTURE BOOKS IN PAPERBACK FROM FRANCES LINCOLN

CHINYE
Obi Onyefulu
Illustrated by Evie Safarewicz

Poor Chinye! Back and forth through the forest she goes, fetching and carrying for her cruel stepmother. But strange powers are watching over her, and soon her life will be magically transformed... An enchanting retelling of a traditional West African folk tale of goodness, greed and a treasure-house of gold.

Suitable for National Curriculum English - Reading, Key Stages 1 and 2
Scottish Guidelines English Language - Reading, Level B
ISBN 0-7112-1052-7 £4.99

LITTLE INCHKIN
Fiona French

Little Inchkin is only as big as a lotus flower, but he has the courage of a Samurai warrior. How he proves his valour, wins the hand of a princess, and is granted his dearest wish by the Lord Buddha is charmingly retold in this Tom Thumb legend of old Japan.

Suitable for National Curriculum English - Reading, Key Stages 1 and 2
Scottish Guidelines English Language - Reading, Levels A and B
ISBN 0-7112-0917-0 £4.99

ANANCY AND MR DRY-BONE
Fiona French

Penniless Anancy and rich Mr Dry-Bone both want to marry Miss Louise, but *she* wants to marry the man who can make her laugh. An original story, based on characters from traditional Caribbean and West African folk tales.

Selected for Children's Books of the Year 1992
Shortlisted for the Kate Greenaway Award 1992
Winner of the Sheffield Book Award 1992, Category 0 - 6 years
Chosen as part of the recommended booklist for the National Curriculum Key Stage 2, English Task 1996: Reading, Levels 1-2
Suitable for National Curriculum English - Reading, Key Stage 1
Scottish Guidelines English Language - Reading, Level A
ISBN 0-7112-0787-9 £4.99

All Frances Lincoln titles are available at your local bookshop or by post from:
Frances Lincoln Books, c/o Bookpoint Ltd, 39 Milton Park, Abingdon, Oxon OX14 4TD.
24 Hour Credit Card Line 01235 831700
To order, send:
Title, author, ISBN number and price for each book ordered.
Your full name and address.
Cheque or postal order made payable to Bookpoint Ltd
for the total amount, plus postage and packing as below.
U.K. & B.F.P.O. - £1.00 for the first book, and 50p
for each additional book up to a maximum of £3.50.
Overseas & Eire - £2.00 for the first book,
£1.00 for the second and 50p for each additional book.

Prices and availability are subject to change without notice.